101 DALMATIANS

Hello! My name is Pongo. I'm the handsome Dalmatian in the picture! This is one of my puppies, and this is my pet, Roger Radcliff.

The story I'm about to tell you began in London, not so very long ago. At that time Roger and I lived in his bachelor flat just off Regent's Park. Roger was a musician of sorts and he so loved his work that he seemed to spend every day at the piano making up songs. But, unfortunately, he wasn't very good at it and life was extremely dull. I felt that we both deserved something more interesting.

I soon came to realise that what Roger really needed was an attractive mate.

One bright sunny afternoon in spring, I took up my usual place at the window overlooking the park. It was full of dogs taking their pets out for a walk. I was bored and wanted to join them, but I knew Roger would never stop writing those awful songs until after five o'clock.

I decided to use the time to look for a suitable companion for us. There were several candidates to choose from... Miss Poodle? No, too snooty, and I was sure Roger wouldn't like her mistress. The Afghan was an unusual breed, but when I saw her mistress I knew she wasn't quite right for Roger.

Suddenly, I caught sight of a most beautiful creature, a Dalmatian like me. She was so lovely that my heart skipped a beat. And her mistress was lovely, too. She would be just right for Roger.

They were heading for the park – a perfect meeting place. I needed to get Roger's attention at once.

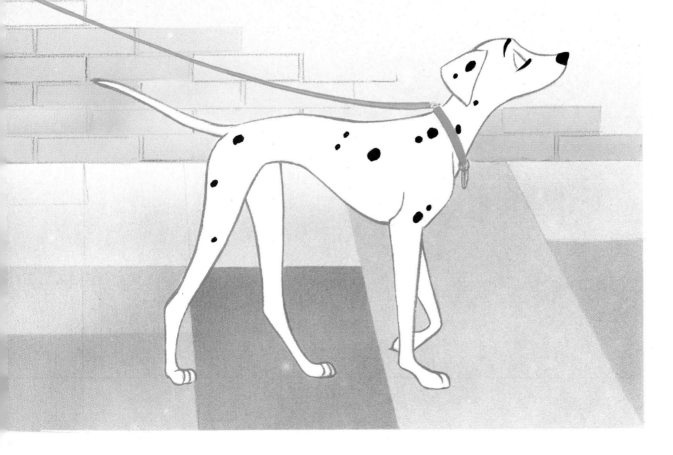

What on earth could I do? Suddenly, I had a brilliant idea. Quietly tiptoeing to the clock, I pushed its hands forward with my paw. I then picked up my lead and ran to the door, barking and wagging my tail furiously.

Roger glanced up at the clock in disbelief. "Time for your walk already?" he said, getting up from the piano.

There was no time to lose. I gave Roger his hat and rushed
to open the door. "Pongo, old boy, take it easy!" shouted Roger,
as I dragged him along the path. "What's all the hurry?"

At first, I was afraid we'd missed them. But then I spotted them sitting by the pond.

By this time Roger had decided to sit down on the grass. I had to do something, so I grabbed Roger's hat and carried it over to the lady. I placed it on the bench where she sat reading. But for some reason she got up and started to walk away, taking the love of my life with her.

13

I started to follow them, but Roger hurriedly caught me by the collar. "Now, come on, Pongo. We're going home," he said firmly, fastening on my lead.

I would not give up that easily. I was determined they should meet. So I dragged Roger towards the lovely pair. As I ran in circles round the lady, she and Roger became entangled in the lead. Then, suddenly… splash! … they fell headfirst into the pond.

"Oh no," I thought. "This means trouble." But, fortunately, I was wrong. The lady, whose name was Anita, started to laugh, and Roger helped her out of the water.

Roger and Anita soon
fell in love and got married.

I was delighted, because I
was in love with Perdita,
Anita's Dalmatian. We all
moved into Roger's cosy
flat and lived happily
together.

But one day, six months
later, our peaceful lives
were shattered. It all began
with a ring of the doorbell.

In walked Anita's old school friend, Cruella De Vil. She was wearing a tight satin dress and fur coat. Perdita took one look at her and crept off to the kitchen.

"Hello, darling!" Cruella cried, waving her cigarette and filling the place with smoke.

Eventually she came to the point of her visit. "Anita, darling," she said, "I've heard that Perdita is expecting little ones. And you know how much I adore puppies. Now promise you'll let me know when they arrive."

Anita hesitated and offered Cruella some tea. But Cruella was already on her way out. "No, I've got to run, darling. Now, don't forget. Cheerio."

Anita and I hated the thought of giving away any of the puppies. We waited anxiously until Roger came downstairs. He found us both wearing such sad faces that he decided to cheer us up. He began dancing with Anita and, before we knew it, we were all dancing and laughing.

I went to reassure Perdita that everything would be all right.

The puppies arrived one wild and stormy night. While Anita was helping Perdita, Roger and I waited nervously outside the room. At last, I heard Anita shout, "The puppies are here!" and I leapt into Roger's lap with delight.

Perdita lay on the cushions with a tired smile on her face. Next to her were five… ten… fifteen small white balls of fluff! I was the proudest father in the world.

"Fifteen puppies!" a shrill voice echoed behind us. "That's marvellous." I looked up to see Cruella De Vil standing in the doorway. She had not forgotten.

"If you are certain they will have their spots in a few weeks, darling, I'll take them all," shouted Cruella, waving her chequebook. "Just name your price!"

Cruella started to write a cheque but her pen wouldn't work. Ink showered everywhere as she shook her pen wildly.

I started to tremble with anger. But Roger, who now had nearly as many black spots as a Dalmatian, was firm. He told her that the puppies were not for sale. Cruella realised that he meant what he said, and she stormed out into the dark night.

The puppies were a real joy to us. As the weeks passed, they grew more lively and their Dalmatian spots started to appear.

They loved to watch television. Their favourite programme was about a dog called Thunderbolt, who was a sheriff's dog in the Wild West.

We used to sit in front of the television each evening. Some of the puppies would climb onto the settee for a better view. Whenever Thunderbolt came on the screen, they would bark with excitement.

27

When the noise became too loud, Nanny would come into the room to investigate. She was the one who looked after us, and she loved the puppies almost as much as we did.

Each night, Nanny would tuck up the puppies safely in their basket in the kitchen. When they were all sound asleep, Perdita and I would take Anita and Roger for an evening stroll.

One night we were so keen to go for our walk that we didn't notice the two men who were watching us from a lorry parked in the street. They waited until we were well out of sight before marching to our front door and ringing the doorbell.

Nanny opened the door.

"Sorry to disturb you, Madam, but we've come to inspect the wiring and switches," said the tall man.

"At this time of night?" Nanny exclaimed. "You're not coming in here. And anyway, there's nothing wrong with the electricity," she said, closing the door.

The two men wouldn't take no for an answer. They pushed the door open and forced their way into the house.

"Don't you dare go up there," shouted Nanny, chasing one of the men upstairs. But he paid no attention.

"If you don't get out of this house, I'll call the police," Nanny continued, as she looked for the man in the attic. Suddenly the door was closed firmly behind her. By the time she had managed to get free, the two men were gone and the puppies were nowhere to be seen.

It was at this point that we arrived home. As soon as Roger heard the terrible news he picked up the phone and called the police.

Early the next morning the phone rang. We waited
eagerly as Anita answered the call. But it was only Cruella
De Vil. She had read about the dog-napping in the
newspapers and wanted to hear every detail from Anita.

"Did she ring to confess?" said Roger, as Anita put down the phone. "She's my number one suspect."

"Roger, I admit she's odd, but she's not a thief," scolded Anita. "Oh, whatever are we going to do?" she sobbed and ran to Roger for comfort.

Suddenly I had an idea. I went to find Perdita, who was lying on the kitchen floor near the empty basket. "Perdy, I'm afraid it's all up to us," I whispered.

Later that night in the open park, I sent out a message on the twilight bark. "Fifteen puppies have been stolen," I called.

After a little while I heard a Great Dane answer me in the distance. Then one dog after another began barking the message across the whole city.

37

The alert spread out into the countryside, passing from farmhouse to farmhouse. Then snow began to fall, muffling the sound of the barking.

Eventually the alert was picked up by Captain, an old farm horse. He and a cat named Sergeant Tibs went to wake the Colonel.

All three listened intently.

"Sounds like a number," exclaimed the Colonel. "Three fives is…"

"Fifteen, sir," replied Sergeant Tibs.

"Yes, I know," said the Colonel. "Fifteen… spotted puddings… no!… puddles?"

They listened again. "Fifteen spotted puppies stolen. That's it!" shouted the Colonel.

Sergeant Tibs scratched his ear. "Colonel, sir, I've just remembered something. Two nights ago I heard the sound of puppies barking at the old De Vil mansion."

"Nonsense, Tibs!" snapped the Colonel. "No one has lived there for years."

"Hold on a moment," said Captain. "There's smoke coming from the chimney."

The Colonel was puzzled. "That's very strange indeed," he said. "Well, I suppose we had better investigate. First, I'll tell the twilight bark to stand by."

Tibs jumped up onto the Colonel's back and off they trudged through the snow.

"Tibs, go and see what's happening," ordered the Colonel when they reached the gate of the deserted mansion. Silently, Tibs climbed up a tree and leapt onto a windowsill. Cautiously, he peeped in through the window.

What a scene! On a settee sat a tough-looking man with a bottle in his hand. Surrounding him were ten, fifteen, twenty, fifty – maybe more – little Dalmatians.

The Sergeant swiftly discovered a hole in the wall and crept into the room. He called softly to the nearest Dalmatian. "Are you one of the fifteen stolen puppies?"

"Oh no, I'm not stolen. I was bought from a pet shop," replied the puppy.

"How about that group of little ones nearest the television?" another puppy whispered. "They have names and collars. They're not from the pet shop, and they only arrived a few hours ago."

"Are there fifteen of them?" inquired Sergeant Tibs.

"I'm not sure. Why don't you count them?" the puppy answered. "But watch out for the Baduns."

"The Baduns?"

"Those two men eating and drinking near the television – Horace and Jasper. They're really horrible."

Tibs tiptoed to the settee and climbed up quietly onto the table behind it so that he could see more clearly. But just as he reached the top, the man moved.

"If I stay perfectly still, perhaps he won't know I'm here," thought Tibs, as he froze beside a wine bottle.

Without looking, the man reached out for the bottle. But instead he grabbed Tibs by the neck. He was about to take a swig when Tibs let out an enormous "MEEOOWW!!!"

Jasper was so stunned that he dropped the cat.

Tibs ran as fast as he could to the hole in the wall. He knew all he needed. He was certain there was a new group of fifteen puppies. He leapt out of the house and went to find the Colonel.

Meanwhile, the twilight bark was hard at work. The Colonel had passed on the news, and the message travelled back to the city. A Great Dane heard it and managed to find us.

"The puppies have been located somewhere north of here. Can you leave tonight?" he asked.

"Yes, yes, of course," I replied. "We can leave right away."

"Good. Here are the directions to the De Vil mansion where the puppies have been hidden."

"De Vil?" repeated Perdy. "Oh, Pongo, it *was* her after all."

We followed the Great Dane's instructions as quickly as we could – but Cruella had driven there before us.

Seeing Horace and Jasper in front of the television, she began to shout. "Get up, you idiots. The police are everywhere. I want the skins of those puppies to make fur coats, and I want them before morning, or there'll be big trouble." She slammed the door so hard on her way out that plaster fell from the ceiling and landed on Horace's head.

Tibs was horrified. He crept out from his hiding place in the wall to warn the puppies. "Quick!" he hissed. "You're in great danger. Follow me and don't make a sound."

The puppies did as they were told and clambered through the hole in the wall. But one of the little Dalmatians was glued to the television, completely unaware of what was going on. Keeping close to the ground, Tibs sneaked silently round the settee and snatched the puppy away.

Just as he pushed the last puppy through the hole, the television programme the Baduns had been watching came to an end, and Horace and Jasper rose from the settee, yawning and stretching.

"Hey, look, Horace," called Jasper. "The puppies have gone!"

At that moment, Perdita and I were crossing the river near Cruella's house. We could hear shouting and loud barking.

"Come on! Hurry!" I cried. "Something must have happened."

Meanwhile, Sergeant Tibs led the puppies down the stairs, looking for a way out. Suddenly they heard Jasper calling from the room above them.

Tibs and the puppies hid under the staircase.

"Shush!" whispered the cat, silencing one of the puppies with his paw. Tibs thought he could hear growling noises outside. "At last," he said. "The others have arrived."

Perdita and I rushed into the mansion and attacked the men. We were so quick that Jasper and Horace were completely taken by surprise. I snapped fiercely at Jasper's feet and knocked him off balance.

"Help, Horace!" he shouted,
as he fell to the floor with a
painful bump.

Horace ran towards the fireplace to snatch the poker. Perdita and one of the puppies grabbed the corners of the rug and pulled hard.

Horace was sent tumbling into the fireplace. "Ouch! Fire!" he yelled and he rushed outside, trailing smoke behind him.

While the fighting was continuing, Sergeant Tibs and the Colonel had led the puppies to a barn.

We joined them later, and were amazed when we saw how many puppies there were. Then Sergeant Tibs explained what Cruella had wanted to do with them all.

"We'll take all the puppies back to London," I said. "Roger and Anita will look after them."

No sooner had we left the building than Jasper and Horace appeared. The Colonel growled loudly in the doorway.

"Look! Paw prints," said Jasper.

"Yes, but where are those little mutts?" replied Horace, who was carrying a big club.

"The tracks lead into the barn. Come on. Let's have a look. They won't get away this time," said Jasper.

The two men walked carefully past the Colonel and entered the barn. Jasper lit a match and began to look inside the haystack.

Neither of the men realised how close they were to the horse's stable. Tibs sat quietly on Captain's back, waiting for a suitable opportunity.

The cat whispered into his companion's ear, "Ready, Captain..." The horse lifted his right hind leg and aimed it at Jasper. "Ready, steady... fire one!" Jasper went flying across the barn. "Fire two!" and Horace suddenly found himself with a mouthful of hay, scrambling in the stack.

Meanwhile, the puppies ran with all their might as Perdita and I led the way through the deep snow. We had to keep stopping to count them to make sure we didn't leave any behind. The smallest one became exhausted after a couple of miles, and I was forced to carry him by the collar. I began to wonder what we would do when the others became too tired to go any further.

As we approached a building in the distance, a collie came out to meet us. "We have shelter for you at the dairy farm across the road," he said. "You can all rest and make an early start in the morning."

"Oh, thank goodness!" I replied and turned to call to Perdita. "This way, Perdy. The farm."

All the puppies suddenly found some extra energy and we headed at once for the warm barn.

The collie opened the barn door and watched the puppies file in one after another. The tired pups flopped down on the dry hay in front of the cows.

"Just look, Queenie," said Princess, one of the dairy cows. "Aren't they adorable!"

"Poor little darlings. They must be starving," mooed Queenie in reply. "We'll give them some fresh, warm milk. That will make them feel better."

When the puppies had drunk all the milk their tummies could hold, they settled down to sleep.

The collie had saved us some scraps of meat. "It's not much," he said, "but it might hold you as far as Dinsford. There is a Labrador in the village there who will be able to help you to get back to London."

Early next day we started on our way again. The crisp snow showed clearly every step we had taken. I told Perdita to run ahead with the puppies whilst I stayed behind to sweep away our tracks. Soon I heard two cars approaching. It was, as I feared, Cruella De Vil and the two dog-nappers. I stood silently and watched Cruella pull up at the side of Jasper and Horace's van.

"This is your last chance, you numskulls!" she screeched. "They must be in Dinsford by now. Get after them at once!"

I found Perdita and the puppies hiding in an empty blacksmith's workshop in the village. We all ducked down as Cruella's car went past the window.

The Labrador who had led them to safety explained that a lorry would shortly be leaving for London, once its engine had been repaired. It was big enough for even a hundred and one Dalmatians – and it meant that we wouldn't have to walk. But how could we get to the lorry without being spotted by the dog-nappers?

I turned to scold two of the puppies who were fighting in the burnt-out fireplace. They were completely covered in soot. But, suddenly I had an idea…

I ran across to the fireplace, jumped into the soot and started to roll around.

"Look, I'm a Labrador," I cried. "If we all roll in the soot, we'll all be Labradors and we can make our way to the lorry without the Baduns spotting us."

"Better hurry," the Labrador panted. "We're running out of time. The lorry is about to leave." I quickly helped the last batch of puppies into their sooty coats, and we ran out into the street.

Cruella's car appeared in the distance. As she drew near, she leaned her head out of the window and looked puzzled as she counted the black Labradors in front of her. The puppies paused, looking scared. "Come on. Keep going," I urged. There was not a moment to spare.

Suddenly our disguise was ruined. Melting snow dripped from the roofs above… revealing large white spots.

Cruella could hardly believe
her eyes. "Horace! Jasper!" she
screamed. "There they go. The
Dalmatians. After them! After
them, you idiots!"

The Baduns rushed up to see
where Cruella was pointing, and
tripped each other up in their
haste to follow us.

We were not far from the lorry now, but we could see that the driver was getting into the cab. Our Labrador friend helped me to lift the puppies into the lorry.

As I thrust the final puppy into Perdita's paws, the driver started the engine and the lorry began to move. I could see the Baduns just a few steps behind me, so I launched myself forward and landed on the lorry's tailgate.

Cruella shook her fist in anger as she watched us disappear into the distance.

Suddenly, we heard her car screech alongside us. She was trying to force the lorry off the road. The driver put his head out of the window and shouted at Cruella. He swerved to enter a single track bridge, leaving his attacker to crash through the railings and into a deep drift of snow.

This made Cruella angrier than ever. She slammed the car into reverse, sending up a huge shower of snow. Part of the bonnet had been damaged, but Cruella was determined to get back onto the road. Flames burst from the engine as she sped up the hill after the lorry. Perdy and I watched with horror as she came closer and closer to us. We heard her accelerate the car, and knew that this time she would ram the rear of the lorry.

"Oh no! Here she comes again!" cried Perdita. "I wish the driver would go faster."

I looked to my left, and gasped. The blue van driven by the Baduns was coming at full speed down the hill, heading straight for us. I closed my eyes and waited for the crash.

We were so lucky! The Baduns were seconds late and missed their target. They crashed into Cruella's car, and Jasper, Horace and the devil woman herself went flying through the air. The last we saw of Cruella she was surrounded by the wreckage of her car, stamping her foot in fury.

Back in London, Anita was trimming the Christmas tree. It looked as if it was going to be a very sad holiday. "Oh, Roger," she sighed, "I still can't believe that Pongo and Perdita would run away."

Nanny entered with some hot chocolate. "Here's a bit of Christmas cheer," she said, "if there's anything to be cheerful about." And she wiped a tear from her eye.

As Nanny started back to the kitchen she heard a faint barking sound. The barks grew louder and louder. Suddenly the door burst open and we charged into the lounge. I bounced on Roger and knocked him onto the floor. Perdy flew towards Anita, covering her in soot.

"Why, it's Perdita! And all the puppies!" Anita cried with joy, wiping the soot from Perdy's face.

Nanny was soon out with the broom dusting off the little puppies, as tears of happiness streamed down her cheeks.

Perdy and I looked on as our pets started to count the puppies. "Thirty-six and eleven, that's forty-seven," calculated Roger.

"And eighteen and thirteen and six," added Anita, "that's eighty-four... plus another fifteen."

"And don't forget Pongo and Perdita," said Nanny.

Roger put his hand to his head. "A hundred and one Dalmatians! Where did they all come from?"

"Whatever shall we do with them?" wondered Anita aloud.

"We'll keep them," Roger replied. "My last song was a great success and earned plenty of money. We can afford to buy a large house in the country."

Perdy and I could hardly believe our ears. Roger went over to hug Anita and together they danced across to the piano. Roger had another inspiration for a song. "I think I'll call it Dalmatian Plantation," he said.

We all joined in and dreamed of our new home in the country – our very own Dalmatian Plantation.

And that is how our story ends – 101 Dalmatians all living happily ever after!